D0590381

First published by Parragon in 2009
Parragon
Queen Street House
4 Queen Street
Bath BA1 1HE, UK

Copyright © 2009 Disney Enterprises, Inc.

All rights reserved. No part of this publication may be reproduced,
stored in a retrieval system or transmitted, in any form or by any means,
electronic, mechanical, photocopying, recording or otherwise, without
the prior permission of the copyright holder.

ISBN 978-1-4075-5830-1
Printed in China

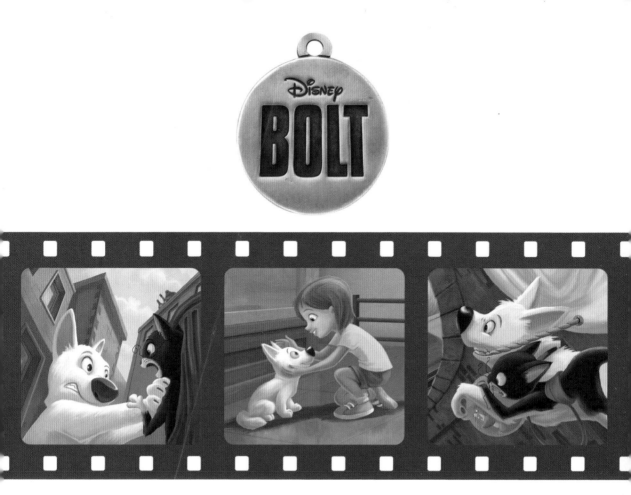

Adapted by
Lisa Marsoli

Illustrated by
Andrew Phillipson and Jean-Paul Orpiñas,
and the Disney Storybook Artists

Designed by
Winnie Ho

Copyright © 2008 Disney Enterprises, Inc.

It was morning at the pet shop. Most of the puppies jumped and yipped, hoping to be adopted. But not Bolt. He continued playing happily, waiting for his special person to find him. Then suddenly, there she was! Bolt sat up straight and wagged his tail – which he couldn't resist chasing.

"You're my good boy," the little girl named Penny said.

Penny's father was a professor, and he had some top-secret scientific information that an evil, green-eyed man named Dr. Calico wanted.

Penny's dad was worried about keeping Penny safe from Dr. Calico. So one night, he took Bolt to his laboratory and changed the pup. From now on, it would be Bolt's job to protect Penny with his amazing powers.

Sure enough, the day arrived when Dr. Calico captured Penny's father. Penny's search for him led her and Bolt to the top of a building. Penny used binoculars to look into a window across the way, and spotted one of Dr. Calico's thugs. He was facing a huge floating screen, talking with Dr. Calico, who was holding Penny's father in his secret hide-out.

Minutes later, Bolt and Penny were on their way to find the villain's hiding place. But suddenly Dr. Calico's troopers came after Penny!

"Bolt! Zoom!" Penny called out. The dog grabbed a leash and pulled her away from the bad guys at top speed. Bolt used all of his super powers to save her, at last resorting to his awesome super bark. It worked! The pavement rippled, the troopers' vehicles toppled, and Penny was safe.

"Good job, buddy," congratulated Penny.

She picked up Bolt and carried him to his trailer. He didn't see the bad guys behind him, getting up unharmed. Bolt didn't know that he and Penny were actors on a TV show! The director thought this would help Bolt be a better actor if he believed his adventures were true.

But even in his trailer, Bolt couldn't relax and play. He was always on the alert to protect Penny. It made Penny sad that Bolt never could have fun like an ordinary dog.

During the next show, Dr. Calico captured Penny in a chamber.
But this time Bolt couldn't save her because an animal handler
was holding him back. The frantic dog was carried away. He had to
save Penny! The first chance he got, Bolt escaped. Something that
looked like the chamber was just outside the window! Bolt leapt
and hit the glass. **SMACK!** He knocked himself out and fell back
into a cardboard box filled with packing peanuts.

Bolt's box was shipped from Hollywood to New York City. When he finally burst out of it, his powers no longer seemed to be working. He thought maybe it had something to do with the packing peanuts.

Bolt continued his search for Penny by questioning a stray cat named Mittens.

"Okay! I know where Penny is!" the terrified cat lied. She pulled a map out of the trash, and showed Bolt that he had to get back to Hollywood.

But how? Bolt needed Mittens to find Dr. Calico – and Penny. Against Mittens' wishes, he tied her to him with a leash, and they got on a moving van headed toward Hollywood. But when Bolt saw some packing peanuts, he jumped off the truck, dragging Mittens with him. He still thought the peanuts weakened him.

They found an RV park and got some food — and met Rhino, a big fan of the Bolt show who lived in a plastic ball.

"You're Bolt! You're fully awesome!" Rhino the hamster cried.

To Rhino's delight, Bolt allowed him to join the mission! The plan was to swing down onto a train and ride it to Penny.

"Every time he did this on the magic box, it was awesome!" Rhino said.

Suddenly, Mittens understood: Bolt played a super-dog on television! But his amazing TV powers weren't real, and the three fell off the train.

Mittens climbed a tree to escape Bolt – but more trouble was on the way. An animal control officer had heard Bolt barking!

The officer grabbed the pair and put them each into separate kennels in his truck. Bolt rammed the cage door, but it wouldn't budge. He wondered if there were any packing peanuts in the truck, weakening him.

Meanwhile, Rhino was rolling along behind the truck. The first chance he got, he unlocked Bolt's door. The dog came flying out and fell into a puddle. As he got up, Bolt noticed his lightning bolt was smeared. He realized that if it wasn't real, his powers weren't real either. Bolt felt terrible. He was just an ordinary dog.

"All right. Now we have to go get the prisoner back," Rhino said to Bolt. The dog hesitated. How could he rescue Mittens without his amazing powers?

But Rhino convinced him, and after a wild chase, Bolt did save Mittens, and all three animals ran from the shelter.

The trio jumped into a house passing by on a truck.

"If I don't chase bad guys, then what am I?" Bolt sadly asked Mittens.

Mittens started showing Bolt how fun an ordinary dog's life was. Then they found Rhino shouting in front of an air vent. Bolt felt the air from the vent and loved it.

Mittens led Bolt over to a window on the moving house and told him to stick out his head and tongue. "This is totally AWESOME!" he shouted into the breeze.

Days passed as the threesome moved from the house to other vehicles headed west. Mittens taught Bolt how to fetch and enjoy normal dog activities. All the while, Mittens was surprised by how much she was learning to trust and like Bolt.

One day, the rain washed away the rest of the lightning bolt on Bolt's side. Bolt the TV star was gone, and Bolt the regular dog had taken his place.

WELCOME

Soon the trio
arrived in Las Vegas,
Mittens was delighted
with all the free food, and
wanted to stay. But Bolt still
wanted to return to Penny.

"There is no Penny! She's
fake!" Mittens argued. But Bolt
still believed in his person. He
set off alone to find her.

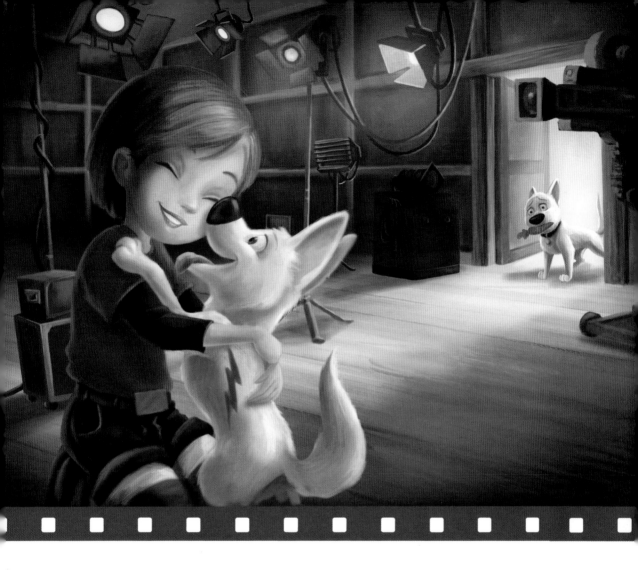

As soon as Bolt arrived at the studio lot in Hollywood, he went to his old soundstage, looking for Penny.

"Bolt! You're okay!" he heard Penny cry. Bolt raced toward the sound of her voice, but saw another dog jumping into Penny's arms!

Bolt slipped away, his heart broken. He didn't realize Penny and the dog were just rehearsing for the show.

When the rehearsal ended, the new dog happily ran to get a treat from his trainer.

But Penny burst into tears. She missed her real Bolt!

Mittens watched Penny crying from up on the catwalk. She and Rhino had followed Bolt to Hollywood.

Mittens raced outside the studio and found Bolt. She had to tell Bolt about Penny. "I saw that girl's face, okay? She's your person. And you're her dog."

Suddenly Bolt's ears shot up. "It's Penny!" he shouted.

Back on the set, a fire had broken out. Everyone fled, not realizing Penny was trapped inside. But the real Bolt knew she was in trouble!

"Just make sure I get in that building!" Bolt shouted to Mittens and Rhino.

A piece of falling debris fell on Rhino. The ball cracked, and Mittens pulled the small warrior free. Bolt dashed by them and into the building. The passage collapsed behind him, leaving Bolt trapped inside.

At last Bolt and Penny were reunited. Then a piece of the set collapsed. In the haze, Penny grabbed a piece of rope and cried out, "Bolt! Zoom!"

The dog found her again and led her to an air vent. Penny could go no farther, but she told Bolt to go. She loved him that much. Bolt looked at Penny and refused to leave without her. He might not be a super-dog, but he was Penny's dog. And then Bolt barked – just a regular bark, but his best bark ever. The sound echoed through the vent, and the firefighters rescued them both.

After that, Penny's family – which now included Bolt, Mittens, and Rhino – left Hollywood and moved to a big farmhouse in the country. Mittens became a pampered house cat, Rhino knew he was just as brave as any action hero he watched on TV, and Bolt got to be a regular dog, playing with Penny to his heart's content.

Bolt knew that once you've found your special person, a dog's life is just about the most perfect life there is.

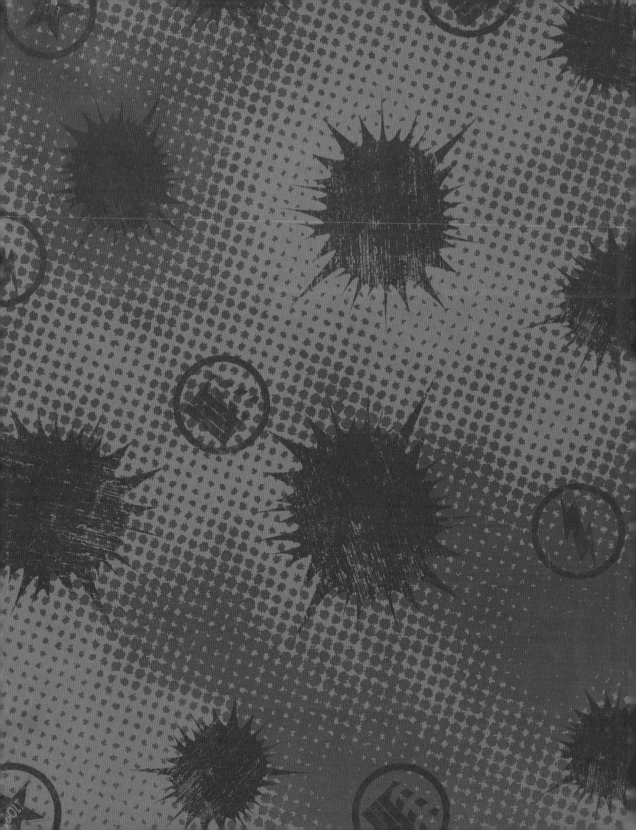